Where's Rusty?

Heather Amery
Illustrated by Stephen Cartwright
Edited by Jenny Tyler

S0-BCA-450

This is Rusty. He lives at Apple Tree Farm.

There is a little yellow duck in every picture. Can you find it?

This is Poppy and Sam.
They are looking for Rusty, their dog.

Poppy and Sam go to look in the shed.

Poppy and Sam stop by the tent.

Ted is working on the tractor.

Poppy and Sam can't find Rusty anywhere.

Poppy and Sam go into the kitchen.

This edition first published in 2003 by Usborne Publishing Ltd., Usborne House, 83-85 Saffron Hill, London EC1N 8RT, England.
www.usborne.com Copyright © 2003, 1997 Usborne Publishing Ltd.

The name Usborne and the devices are Trade Marks of Usborne Publishing Ltd. All rights reserved.
No part of this publication may be reproduced, stored in a retrieval system or transmitted in any form or by any
means, electronic, mechanical, photocopying, recording or otherwise without the prior permission of the publisher.
UE
Printed in Singapore
First published in America August 1997